The Bad Babies' Counting Book

A Beaver Book

Published by Arrow Books Limited

62-5 Chandos Place, London WC2N 4NW

An imprint of Century Hutchinson Ltd

London Melbourne Sydney Auckland
Johannesburg and agencies throughout the world

First published by Piccadilly Press 1985

Beaver edition 1987

Printed and bound in Great Britain
by Scotprint, Musselburgh, Scotland

ISBN 0 09 946310 5

The Bad Babies' Counting Book

Tony Bradman

Illustrated by Debbie van der Beek

Beaver Books

One bad baby,
bouncing on his bed,

Two bad babies,
with their breakfasts on their heads.

2

Three bad babies,
on their way to school,

Four bad babies fighting –
that's against the rules!

Five bad babies,
drinking from their cups,

5

Six bad babies,
in the bathroom cleaning up.

6

Seven bad babies sulking,
with faces very long,

7

Eight bad babies singing,
what a lovely song!

8

Nine bad babies,
outside having fun,

9

Ten bad babies bawling,
loudly, every one.

10

But some bad babies
like helping at the shops,

And some bad babies
think that bath time is the tops . . .

Two bad babies,
love the book that they've just read,

And here's one bad baby —
still bouncing on his bed!